Love Covers
All Things

From the author:
I hope you will all enjoy reading these as
much as I enjoyed writing them

Crumps Barn Studio
Crumps Barn, Syde, Cheltenham GL53 9PN
www.crumpsbarnstudio.co.uk

Cover design and illustrations by Lorna Gray

Printed in Gloucestershire on FSC certified paper by Severn, a
carbon neutral company

ISBN 978-1-915067-10-4

Love Covers
All Things

BEVERLEY GORDON

Collected Poems

Crumps Barn Studio

FRANKENSTEIN LOVE

Where are you my love?
I cannot see you.
Oh my love, it's so dark in here. I am scared.
Hush now, I am here. Not long now, the light will
     come again

Ah yes my love the light has come again
It shines so bright oh my love can you see it?
Not yet, describe it to me.

Where are you my love?
I cannot feel my arms.
Hush now not long to go soon you'll be holding me

Where are you my love?
I cannot feel my leg. Oh my love I am scared.
Hush now my love, soon you'll be walking again

Oh my love where can you be?
My heart keeps missing a beat, I am going to need surgery
Oh my love where can you be? I spend months searching
      for thee
Oh my love where can you be? I am dying, can't you see?
Oh my love oh my love what's happening to me?
I can feel my heart going to sleep.
Oh my love is this the end of me?
Where can you be?

Pause. A deep breath, I take.
Oh my love you have revived me.
Where have you been?

I have been here all the time
But there was a block to your heart line, I could not get
      close to thee
Then I heard you cry in despair
It took all the strength I had to unblock your heart line
But your heart was too weak, so I gave you mine.

Oh my love, oh my love
Oh my love, you have saved me
Hush now I am tired, can't you see? There is not much
     left of me.
My last gift to thee.
Now live my love for both of we
Oh my love, you are now part of me.

How far would you go for the one you love?

WHO ARE YOU
TALKING ABOUT

You see me at my worst, you see me at my best
I have been used, I have been abused
I have been broken, I have been mended, I have been
      lied to.
I have been called all sort of names
I have been the cause of everything broken, so they
      claim
Who am I?
I am the one that catches you when you fall
I am the one that is always by your side
I am the one that makes everything right
I am the one that causes you no harm, the one you trust
      to do what's right
I am the one that makes you feel safe and holds
      back your tears
I am the one that holds you tight

I am the one that mends your heart
I am the one that forgives and forgets
You still want to know who I am!
I am just love. Who did you expect?

A BROKEN HEART CAN
BE MENDED

They say a broken heart can mend
Gentle love treat me kind
Gentle love do not leave me behind

An Angel of love you were sent from above
To guide me through the darkest days when the storm
    comes my way
You were there to shelter me out of harm's way
Gentle Angel of love when night falls you light my path

Gentle Angel of love when a fight broke out you stood
    in my way
To take the blow that would put me on the floor
Gentle Angel of love you became my conscience to
    keep me straight
Gentle Angel of love you gave me butter, cream cake
    and a bun.

Gentle Angel of love you quench my thirst with a
      refreshing kind of love
Gentle Angel of love you guide me on the right road that
      only you know
Gentle Angel from above, do you have a name, or should
      I just call you LOVE?

RIGHT PLACE WRONG TIME

A crowded room I was in, my eyes did not blink
For there you were at a distance, but not too far,
    with a super grin
Was there noise in the room? I did not notice for my
    ears were not tuned in
My heart became a piano playing classical melodies
My body became a tambourine of hallelujah, hallelujah
My eyes were truly fixed on the prize.

Oh! Hold the phone, step on the brakes, there were
    obstacles in my way
My prize was slipping, so I turned and walked away.
But my heart was still playing that classical melody
    in low key
My body was the tambourine of hallelujah at low speed
I had no control. I must resist, my soul would
    not let go

Try I might, that obstacle was always still in sight
Ah alas, what was or could have been a
    beautiful symphony
A trumpet, a drum beat that could be jazz melody
It was a prize that was out of my reach
That flame of love still burning dimly but not out.

Psst! this is where you play the violins for all I have
        is memory
Of what could have surely been.

IMPOSSIBLE LOVE

If love is what it takes, I'll do it
If love is what is needed, I'll do it
If love makes you happy, I'll do it
If loves make you run a mile, I'll do it
If love dries your tears, I'll do it
If love makes you reach for the stars, I'll do it
If love catches the cloud and puts it in a jar, I'll do it
If love sings you a sweet song, I'll do it
If love takes you on a journey, I'll do it
If love carries you on its wings to meet the moon
Ooh hold on! If that's all love is to you, I won't do it.

Why can't we share a bag of hot chips under the stars
        on a cold winter night?
Or walk along the sandy beach with the sand
        between our toes,
Before the tide comes in and the moon looks as if it's
        going beneath the sea.
Love doesn't have to be sparkle and glamour if we
        can't afford it, does it?
A good love is just being me and you being you
Being together enjoying each other's company.
Down to earth love is what I would call it.

LOVE IN EVERY LAND

Love is in the air, love is in every land
Looking for love is like looking for the end of a rainbow –
  it's a circle

Love is in the air, love is in every land
Diving into love is like diving into quicksand
And down you go

Love is in the air, love is in every land
Looking for love is not where you start but
  where you finish
You decide

Love is in the air, love is in every land
Searching for love is like sieving the seabed
You might get lucky if the sharks don't get you instead

Love is in the air, love is in every land
Blink and you will miss it
Do you see love? You blinked

Are you actually listening to what I am saying?
LOVE IS IN THE AIR
You cannot dig for it
You cannot search for it
You cannot sieve for it
You cannot trace it
True love will find you which ever land you are in.

MY CONSCIENCE AND ME

Me: I have a secret

C: What is it

Me: It's a secret

C: Then please tell me

Me: I cannot tell me for I am me

C: Here we go again, ok please do tell

Me: Tell what

C: You said I have a secret

Me: Do you? Oh please tell

C: No, no, you have a secret

Me: Do I? Please tell

C: Tell what

Me: My secret

C: If I did, it would not be a secret

Me: But it's not a secret

C: What?!!

Me: A secret is not a secret if you say you have a secret
        For I know you have a secret

C: Do I? Who says I have a secret?

Me: You did – you said I have a secret

C: Do you? Please tell

Me: Tell what

C: Your secret. You say I have a secret

Me: Do you? Please tell

C: Tell what

Me: Your secret

C: My head hurts. I have to give this some thought

Look people a secret is not a secret if you say you
    have a secret
For now everyone knows you have a secret and they
    want to know your secret

I GIVE A REASON,
YOU ASK WHY

I love you not because I want to but because I have to
Why?
I love you not because I need to but because I want to
Why?
I love you not because I have no choice but because
        I have a choice
Why?
I love you not because you tell me to but because
        you force me to
Why?
It does not matter what I say you still want to
        know why, why?
Turn me off
Why?
Oh you horrible person
Why?

My phone and I.
Got you hahaha
Why?

NATURE AT ITS BEST

Yes, my friends another glorious sunshine day
Just let me pull up a chair along this roadside
Observing nature at its best

Nothing like a good sunshine to bring out that smile
It sets peace in one's mind
So what can I see from this busy street
People, cars, animals. Oh my, it going to be a busy day
Let's break it down if you please
Cars driving by, different colours different style
Convertible, not much of that must be too hot
Still they are in such a hurry cannot wonder why.

As the ladies pass by, some dress to impress
Whiles others, modesty is not of their interest
Wrong bras size or none at all
Ah yes, gentleman flexing their chests
with muscles sticking out of their vest
One size too small I expect
Shorts so tight, did they borrow their little brother's size?

Yes, a beautiful day to watch nature at its best
Mothers pushing prams, babies in distress
The bus driver crams everyone in like sardines in a can
Now there is a traffic jam
Frustration sets in, the horns begin to blow
Poor old man trying to cross the road
Why don't they ever use the traffic lights?
The beggars are in between a performance of need
And looking hungry and unclean
Then they go behind the trees counting their coins
        looking pleased
Yes it's a good day to watch nature at its best
Little Harry has dropped his lollypop, wait for it, a
        tantrum is about to begin
Oh dear mother do not yell, just give him another
        if you please
This is too much I must take my leave

I AM HUMAN AFTER ALL

Why do you look down on me?
Is it because I am not clean?
I have no home to call my own, I sometimes have to
        share a bed
Where many strangers have already laid their head,
But they are just like me.
I do have a story to tell, but who would listen to me.

You know I often wonder what it would be like
To soak in a hot bath and feel the steam on my face
And bubbles between my toes, even to lie in a bed with
        white cotton sheets
A bed so big and soft, not needing to share.
And to feel the white cotton pillowcase against my face
That fresh smell of happiness
And to wake up with the sunshine beaming on my face

I often wonder what it is like having hot breakfast
        around a large table
With white linen cloth and fresh flowers and a bowl of
        fruits on display
I often walk by the beautiful homes with flashy cars and
        electric gates
Even hotels that cost a year's mortgage to sleep in their
        bed.

I wonder what's it's like to have a roof over my head
To shelter me from the rain, wind and cold
Ah yes a room to call my own
But I do have that.
It's only a cardboard box hidden under bramble bushes
        but that's my home
I don't pay rent, my neighbours are not nice
The little rats, they're always trying to get in my box
Mr Fox sometimes passes by
He just stops and stares, probably wondering why
But I give him a little of what I got.
I once found a cheeky cat sleeping in my box
But just like me he too would like a home with a cosy
        blanket
To snuggle in, so we keep each other company

In the morning we rise and go our separate ways until
        we meet in the evening
He brings me a dead rat I give him little of what I've got
We talk through the night I tell him about my day
Oh I did not eat the rat in case you are thinking

I often catch the rain to give my face a wash
I may not have a soft pillow or white cotton sheet
But my box is often cosy and warm

I go to the supermarket, I sit outside with a little box, I
        have a note it reads:

I have a home to call my own. It's under a tree, it's a box I
        share with a wild cat
I ask you if you please – no cash – just a tin or two to share
        with the cat
A job I would accept but no one is offering me that.

Not everyone is unkind, some even give me cash I don't
        mind that
In winter I buy a sleeping bag to cosy up
While I give the wild cat his own little private box
        and a blanket
He's cosy in that

While you sip your hot cocoa and cosy up by your
        fireplace
And watch your 50inch TV screen or stare at the ceiling
I don't have the luxury of cocoa but I do have a lukewarm
        mug of tea
I try to be posh and keep my little pinky finger pointing
        in the air
As I gaze up to my million large-size screen
I see the moon, the stars, it's so bright, I cannot tell you
        how many I try to count
For each night is never the same
There are times when I look up the colour of the night
It's a breathtaking sight

So I smile and close my eyes and pray
Thanking those who have always filled my little box
And forgive those who did not.
For they won't be seeing me again. My eyes are tired
My body is extra cold tonight shivering as I am
I know I don't have long to go
I take my last breath, a smile, here I lay.

TRUE FRIENDSHIP

Wow, really how wonderful
Happy for you, so proud of you
These are some of the words that true friendship brings
There is no jealousy, no eyes that are red like the moon
On certain nights

A true friendship holds you close to their heart
And wants the best for you
They encourage you in every possible good way

True friendship is like having a bowl of hot soup on a
    cold winter's day
True friendship brings out the best in you, like a warm
    summer's day

True friendship is like spring-time flowers
that makes you smile and are not far off
When autumn leaves fall and you feel your energy
    slipping away
True friendship slips in and brightens up your day

True friendship will not let you go astray
They keep your feet firmly on the ground
Their time is precious yet they will take a little of it
To help you in any possible way
Oh yes, my dears, that is true friendship and much more.

A BEGGAR HAS SOMETHING TO SAY

I am a beggar, he says
I am a beggar, she said
We rise early, head to the street while others are still fast
    asleep

Hoping for someone to give us a helping hand or even
    something to eat
Many do not understand the life of a beggarman or
    women

It's not our fault we fall into difficulty, unforeseen
    circumstances
We were not born this way. We had an education
Some more than others
We are just one of the unfortunate ones
But who can predict the future of a man or woman?

Can they blame the past on the man we voted for to run
    our land
Or the parents who really did not understand?
Or the bank and landlord who did not want to know
When jobs were no more? Or the country that many were
    forced to run from
There are many reasons behind every story

Begging is not easy, it's hard work you must understand
We put aside pride and deal with the pain as we are
        spit upon.
For each day we face uncertainty

Tell me please where in the world can you go and see a
        lazy beggar
We are judged unfairly
You have many that sit around all day long waiting for
        pay day as they call it free money
They drink and smoke it away
Some finds the betting shop and spend their cash
Wasting it away a horse or two they must play
They don't mind for they know there is another payday
They just roll out of bed any time of the day run and
        cash their cheque
Spit on us on the way, "Go get a job" they would say

People of today accept their way
Yet people of today look down on us beggars who
        rise early
To do our job, yes that's right, being a beggar is not an
        easy way – come to think of it, don't you too have
        a job? Yet you would call on your neighbour next
        door to beg a cup of sugar or two or to borrow a
        couple of quid. How different are we then, for what
        you earn is still never enough to keep sugar in your
        cup and quids in your pockets

We do not earn enough to pay our taxes, it's hard even to
        get a meal for the day
We neither steal from your shop
We have no home the hostels are always packed

A side alley or a phone box even outside a shop
        we call home
But even then the shop keeper would come and say
        "Go away get a job"
Or call the police to move us on
But we are an advantage to his shop
For no one would try to break in to steal his living
So really it's a free service to him that he cannot see

No one really stops to talk to us
Yes I do agree there are beggars who really are not
      beggars at all
Those ones make it hard for us who are genuine
Those who have will go so low to steal the very food
      from our bowl
Some even steal from our pan
But please it can be hard to tell us apart for many
      disguise it so well
So even if you see us, even if you don't want to give us
Please do not turn your noise up on us, spit at us, or
      curse us
You never know there may be an Angel among us
      testing your kindness.

DEPRESSED SOUL

You feel lost among the crowd as everyone is busy
    walking by
Pushing and shoving without a care
Try as you might, you find your situation getting deeper
    and deeper
As if you are slipping away

You wake each morning a start of a new day
But all you want to do is lie there and let the world
    pass away

As hard as you try, your situation gets deeper and deeper
You think you would spend some cash –
    that will cheer you up
But the situation does not go away

You refuse to admit you are depressed, you will not
    ask for help
You say to yourself it's just a situation
When asked, you say I am alright
But really your situation you have left so long it has
    got out of hand

Yet you still deny you have a problem
For you have everything under control
The pressure of life has taken its toll

You have the weight of a donkey load carrying around
     all day and night
But the alternative has not presented itself
Or did it? You could have missed it

For you are weighted down under this heavy load
Each time you awake you go through your routine
Wash your face comb your hair put on clean clothes
     add a false smile
Hoping no one will know or see your pain
Forgetting those who know you so well they can see
     through you
But cannot get over that line
Try as they might yet they have not given up
They wait and watch desperately wanting to act
Force you they cannot
So they wait doing what little they can to keep hold of
     your hand.

A SPECIAL REQUEST

My darling, my husband (alternatively you can use wife)
my sweetheart, my dearest, my love, my best friend
These are just titles, words or expressions
Do they mean anything, let's see ...

My darling – someone close to me
My husband – the ring that you placed on my finger
        when I said "I do"
My sweetheart – all of the times this heart has
        been broken
        You came along and sealed it with a kiss.
My love – unconditionally you gave me
My best friend – always ready to listen and encourage

Throughout our friendship as we started out as friends
OK I must confess I did not take kindly to you for where
        you came from
As I once said to a friend "leave him where he is"

Wow!! was I Foolish,
For I did not know it then but look how far I have come
Twenty-four years and still going strong

So yes, those titles mean something – for you are all of
        the above and much more.

In Jamaican, as you are a fan
It goes like this:
You are my spices in my rice and peas
You are my coconut in my soup
You are my tamarind sometimes sour sometimes sweet
Hey roll with it
Each morning, I wake to find you next to my heartbeat

Thank God I was not too foolish to realise what was in
        front of me
Love you baby.

24 years and still going strong

WHERE ARE YOU RUNNING TO

Are you running?

Maybe

Hmm how far will you run?

I do not know

Do you know the world is a circle just like the sun?

And so?

Well then how can you run, are you not circling the sun
　　Please come now rest up a little, tell me,
　　　　let me understand
　　What is it you are running away from

OK then

Go ahead you have my attention

As a child growing up, I wanted to be a sailor. I wanted to
Have my own boat to take me on my adventure
Around the world I would go

But I could not see any clear way of my destiny
The more I grew, I wanted so much more
I even wanted to put God on hold
But that was not meant to be, I needed a balance
     as you can see

For the world was bigger than me
God opened my eyes so I could see
But still I craved for that adventure, a bird so free

Then what happened?

Love
My eyes were blinded by a beauty that shined before me
My heart began to race, love took first place
Now I had my company, adventure here we come

Ooh!!

Yes Ooh!
Years passed, I began to realise
My adventure seemed to be put on hold
But my love she had grown cold

I began to notice things were not right
But I could not let love go, love had me bang to right
I had no place to run or hide, I knew thing were really
      not right

Why?

It's like this:
I gave my all, she gave me nothing
But love still had a hold on me, I wanted to let go
I was trapped
So I ran away to clear my head
The more I ran I did not want to stop or go back
But the pain is still so great my right arm aches
I cannot turn back for it was just a trap

My mind is fighting against my heart
I am so confused they are tearing me apart

OK I can see your difficulty

For her part, I did not hear. I can only go by
        what you say
Do you understand?
So let me say this
Love has the sweetest kiss, the sweetest talk to
        capture one's heart
For some it's just a game with the intention to win

Samson and Delilah, a story of long ago
Samson loved God but love for another took over his
        heart and tore him apart
OK maybe that's not a good illustration,
        after all she set him up
He was betrayed and she got paid
I am no expert to give advice, all I can say is this:

You had already set out your plan
But found a companion who gave you the impression
That she loved your adventure plan
She agreed to please
But did you tell her it was a lifetime plan ambition?

Well not in so many words but she would know

Come on be a man, take your stand
Ask her about her intentions
She too may have her own adventure plan
Don't assume don't misunderstand
Her heart may have another plan

Starting a family may be one.

Come on don't run away, that problem will not
        go on it's own
For she may well like your plan, but you never
        asked for hers
Nor of her hand or even asked of her own intentions

The only way is to talk it out
Don't ASSUME. Take off the ume you will get ass.

Oh, I see. So you want me to go back and speak

You got that right
For then you will truly know.
By the way did you leave a note?

Aah no!

Then clearly, she does not know.

MY SON, MY SON, A FATHER'S WORK IS NEVER DONE

Father can we speak? I'm troubled, I feel I have anxiety
Pull up a chair take a seat now what's troubling you
    my son

Life has brought me many joys and some tears
I have yet to travel
I have not found what I am searching for

What is that?

I don't know yet I kept looking not really searching
A love I have not yet found
There are many things in the world I want to discover
There are many things I want to do
A new horizon is awaiting me
But I know the family needs me

Oh! Father I need to find me
I don't want my family responsibility

My son I understand how you feel
But this world is bigger than you and me
It's far bigger than the eyes can see

I know you want to discover what lies beyond
But there are hidden dangers that many do not see
My son as I watch you grow, I have kept you close to me
To guide you through the world's obstacles
The danger that lies beneath
How far ahead can you see, you have not yet begun to see
The hidden danger waiting for you

I know you want to be free, but I keep you close so you
         can learn from me

I am confused, I really do not know what to do
Life is so complicated

I know my son, I know
The choices you make will affect the rest of your life

Let me tell you a story my son
A young man loved the sea he felt so free

He wanted no responsibility he wanted to discover
        life just like you
When he was on the boat away from dry land,
The coolness of that warm breeze blowing
        against his cheek,
He wanted to be that fish that swims endlessly

No worries, not a care, just swimming in the warm
        night air
But a voice he did hear shouted loudly
Ooh!! My son, can you not see that great white shark
Waiting to devour you
Come now take a seat, reason with me
As he sat, the voice began to reason with him, for
        this boy was
Determined to be free and forget his responsibility
He put his life at risk, danger was his middle name
Did he really love life, for he liked to take risks
He wanted to live life to the fullest
He followed the saying you only live once
This boy followed his heart he did not care
The voice continued to plead with him
Come now sit here

You set the time on everything, you do –
        you set the number of years
All that I give you is what I can teach you
All that you see in this world at the
        moment is fading away
Soon the sun will not set beyond the horizon
And the moon will be no more

The boy replied:
I hear you loud and clear

But I cannot still help wondering
When will these thing be
For they seem so far way I have to enjoy my life
        while I have the days
Why do I need to take on so much family responsibility
Please forgive me for I have no right to question thee

There there my son, wait patiently
I have put before you knowledge, wisdom,
        faith and discernment
I did not say it would be easy

I hear that but for me I don't need any responsibility
I need to think of me

Will you hold me accountable for the choices
Of wrong that you make
Or will you continue to acquire wisdom, knowledge
A gift I gave

Then the voice went away.

So my son you have a choice

You made that choice to have a wife and a family
You still have the responsibility to do the thing that's right
Yet you set your heart to be free

Father what become of the boy did he do right
And the voice did it come again
I have so many questions I want to know more

Son you are holding his hand
As for the voice
Here a gift for you read this

What! Father, this very old book!

It contains the do's and don'ts and reasons
        and whys of life
And that voice is contained inside
For if I had paid attention, life for me would
        not be this way
Don't make the same mistake
Now guide me inside, alright
My Son, will you come again?

Yes Father, I will come again.

FAMILY FUN DAY

Hey! kids come out and play
It's going to be a family fun day
Pass me the ball, I will throw it your way
Run now, quick, get to first base
Grandpapa move your, excuse me, get out the way

Watch your mouth, I am not too old to play
Have I ever told you the very first time I hit first base

Yes Grandpapa that story has already been told

Now pass them the bat and you try to catch
Where is Grandmama?

She has been up all night baking bread so she is resting
her sleepy head

Where is everyone?

Well Uncle is stuck in the can
Mum and Dad have gone to the supermarket
Aunty is talking to the neighbour again over the fence
I think she likes him but isn't she too old

Young man, watch your mouth
Did I tell you the time I met your Grandmama

Yes Grandpapa many times

How much is many times?

I don't know, I suppose 9

Well then let's make it an even 10
Come on, gather round there are not many of us to play
    ball

You see I had a very hard day at work
It was very late and it begin to rain heavily
As I was driving home, tired I was,
My eyes became very sleepy

That night my car lights were not too bright so it was a
    struggle to see
Then I slammed on the brakes. I looked through my
    windscreen
A figure I saw before me
Wet she was, I offered her a lift

Your back tyre is flat she said
Get in, there is a garage up ahead I said
Then my engine would not start
That was all I needed, I was so angry

"Pop the bonnet" she said
I stared so hard
She repeated "pop the bonnet"
She fixed my car and changed my tyre

But Grandpapa why did you not do it yourself

I did not want to get wet beside she was already wet
I thought if I played my cards right, I'd have my own
        personal mechanic
The money I saved from not taking my car to the garage,
        I bought her a meal

So what happen next
Did Grandmama fall for that?

I thought you didn't want to know?
Let's go inside – time for tea.

IF YOU DON'T MIND

No I don't want a drink
I just want to sit here and think
Sometimes you have to get away
Find a place where you can get lost in your head
I have taken a hundred steps then got in a lift
Press button number 9 to the executive suite
That I may be out of reach to have some peace
My heart rate rises but never skips a beat
I look out ahead, what can I see
To the right of me tall lush green trees
Then to my left concrete jungle from hell
No one could tell that this is a city I am in
Yet it is just like people – divided
So, if you don't mind, I do not want a drink
No phone calls please. I need to think

THROUGH THE EYES OF A?

You just want to die
There are those that refuse to play by the rules
Here is one
It's so hard, too many rules and half of them don't
        make sense
No matter where you go there are rules

Think for a moment. If there were no rules what
        would the world be like
What would your life be?
Are you telling me you want to throw your life away
Just because of rules

Listen to me, a question I will ask of you
Will you cross a busy street where there are
        no traffic lights?
No.
Would you fly in a plane where the pilots did
        as they pleased?
Noo.
If I put you in a car, hand you the key and say drive
        full speed no rules apply
What would you say?
Hmm I have to think about that it's tempting
But noo

Then why not
One I could be killed or I kill some one

So you do love life
Well. Yes
Then why do you want to throw it away?
Too many rules my life seems to be governed by
        rules after rules

Rules are there for a reason. They protect you,
        safeguard you
But you still have a choice if you choose to obey or not

Look the world is not always going to be this way
Yes there will be rules that you will clearly understand
But it will not be so cramped that you cannot move

So while you stand here ready to fall
First look around you. What do you see?

I do not care I want to be free

Ah you are mistaken for you won't be free
You be in a place so damp and cold with only the worms
    to keep your company
And enjoy a midnight feast courtesy of you

Say what!
Look I am keeping it real, come with me take my hand
Why?
For I want you to see so come now spend some time in
    my company

Where are you taking me
I am going to show you the reason why you truly don't
    want to die
Come let's go.
I do not control your mind
I do not control your eyes
I do not control your time
I do not control your feet
You set the time on everything you do
For now you have a choice
Love. Live life
Love – for the greater good
Life – for a future surpassing many years
Live – because I want you to, but you've got to
    want it more

Now can you see all that I have shown you?
Rules allow you to enjoy life to the full.
So what if you did not get that part in the play

I hear you loud and clear
I want to live, to enjoy these things you put before me
I want to love for the greater good of what is to come
I want life surpassing many years

Can I go to school now?
It's too late we have taken today to explore
So, tomorrow for sure
Now no more climbing trees to jump to the ground
No, no I will not do that anymore

TAKE A CHANCE OR NOT

The chance you miss in life can hug your memory
So tight. For many would say you only have one life
While a cat has nine, so the saying goes
That theory was never tested and I hope it will never
    will be

Love endured all things
But it in itself can bring pain that not all can endure
Not all are strong to have the standard of love
Not all are strong to carry the burden of love
Not all are strong to forgive love
Curse is love some would say, for it has only brought
    them sorrow and pain

But did it really?
Or was it the choices that they made
You have the butterfly of love
The lust of love
The desire of love
The want to know what's it like to love
Fantasy of love
But the dark side of love? You don't want to be
    transported there

Failings to recognise true love real love
The love that covers all things
The loves that is forgiven
The secrets it does not reveal
Free spirit of love
Love that you can't hold onto unless you are pure in heart
That sees the good in one despite their flaws.
It's an emotion that brings out the good,
      that stirs up the desire
To do right by others
True Love doesn't look out for its own interests

Keep an open mind
Not all love is what it seems.

DAY DREAMER

Dressed in his cocktail suit, his dicky bow tie
As the black figure of a tall handsome man enters
    the room
His eyes dark and mysterious

Then he turns and smiles
And says "hello!"

His dark eyes engage with mine
He lights up my smile as his deep voice gets me
    weak at the knees
I cannot speak
His beard shines when the light hits his face
His body is so well shaped I avert my eyes
Trying not to be hypnotised
His arms so strong.

Then he says "my name is Ted, do you come here often?"
What a cheap pick-up line. The smile drops from my face
What happens next?

I do not know, for Mum
Throws a bucket of water over me and tells me
To turn off the television and go wash up the plates.

About the Author

Beverley Gordon is the author of four poetry collections: *My Very Tree, Letters From Your Neighbour Far Away* and its sequel *From Your Neighbour In A Distant Land,* and *Love Covers All Things.*

She is a mother and grandmother, and lives and works in London.